AF349393

A difficult case for detective Green

Joan de Jesús Yánez Nuez

ISBN: 978-84-615-3801-0

Depósito legal: GC 495-2011

Thanks to Manuel, my philosophy teacher,
Magali and Miguel and their sons.

The bedroom was untidy, as if it was a bear's burrow or another ferocious criature that could withstand the zone extreme climate.

It was Monday morning and Violette was stunned. She couldn't remember anything happened the night before, at his uncle Dunkan's party, at his mansion. Couldn't almost say a word and extremely distressed, she said to his brother:

-        It's your fault, I told you that coming to our uncle's mansion in this village wasn't a good idea.

- Rejecting his birthday party invitation was unacceptable – Brandon argued.

Once they were standing and slightly calmed, they started to walk along a big ancient gallery where the large windows, situated in front of the spiral staircase, let them see the weak sunlight coming in. In the distance, you could see The Rocky Mountains and just on the right, there was a greenhouse. It was full of endemic species and many other exotic species, typical of other hotter parts of the world. It was the case of the Argentinian chorisia, characterized by a sort of thorn that goes around its always straight trunk.

Suddenly, a scary bloodcurdling cry was heard. It came from downstairs.

- Do we go downstairs? – Violette asked with hesitation and fear.

- What for? I'm exhausted and I don't want to spend my energy. It must be one of the guests making a racket to draw attention of oneself – Brandon asked while he was going again to his bedroom to have a rest.

Brandon is a boy who will be twenty four next September. He has just finished his dregree in Economics and Business Administration and he's already the second biggest shareholder of a renowned company of perfumery and cosmetics, which is managed by Dunkan. He combines his work with his biggest passion: sports. Seeing him playing golf or tennis, some of his favourite activities, is not strange. A little insecure and sometimes spoiled, it coulb be said that he has everything despite being so young. He's got a well-off life, a developing career, a beautiful girlfriend and money to spend. Being the youngest, he had achieved much more than Violette thanks to his good nose in business and, why not, to his impetuosity.

- Do whatever you want, but I'm going to the kitchen to have something for breakfast- Violette said.

- Oh, my god! – the gardener Bob exclaimed, who was in that

moment at the rear of the house, adjoining to the garden, the greenhouse and the swimming pool.

Bob is an environment and nature enthusiast although he has been a firefighter for almost thirty years in Los Angeles fire department, where cinema is synonim of excellence. He used to feel quite well there because he used to go to its beautiful famous beaches in his free time. However, a firefighter's life is not too long as when you are a certain age and you start to lose your fitness, the only option is to leave the job. Thanks to the knowledge that he learnt from his grandfather when he was younger, Bob decided to go to Ruslake and look for a job where he met Dunkan by chance. They both were at the local market; Bob was trying to get an unqualified job to live and the old man looking for the perfect bunch. Dunkan wanted to surprise Margueritte, his wife, with the best bunch he could find. It was their twenty-third wedding anniversary and the thing his wife loved the most was a present coming from the nature. As Dunkan was doubting, Bob approached and introduced himself. Then, he suggested the old man the best products on the flower stall and the instructions he should follow to look after the bunch. That was when Dunkan realized he needed a gardener at home to help Margueritte with their garden.

Violette approached with impetuosity towards the gardener and she saw his uncle lying on the floor.

- Oh, my god! What has happened? – Violette asked.

- Eh... it's... I, I... I've just found him on the floor when I was coming from cutting the grass – Bob replied as he took a deep gust of air.

- But, what the hell is this? What's happening? – the cook Steve, the butler Rodríguez and the cleaning lady said at the same time. They, model loyal workers, were doing their daily tasks; Steve, helped by Rodríguez, was cooking and preparing breakfast and Miss Carrol was hooving the red elegant carpet that is around the house, from the main entrance to the attic, passing by the rooms on the second floor.

- My uncle! – Violette exclaimed very affected as she approched.

- Stop! Don't even touch him! – Bob exlaimed. You cannot touch him, it's one of the first things they taught me at the firefighter department. You shouldn't touch the corpse in order to not to change the scene or the instruments of the crime – said grabbing her.

- He was such a good person – Rodríguez, awkward by the crime, murmured.

- He always treated us kindly – Miss Carroll whispered.

- I'll call the police – Bob said.

Violette started going upstairs sighing and sobbing to let her brother know about it. He had stayed in his bedroom to have a rest, from where you see the nearby village, full of gothic fronts, where vehicles couldn't operate since it was entirely pedestrian. In fact, when they arrived to the mansion they had to do it on foot. Violette didn't relish that idea because she was used to the comforts of living in a big city.

- Brandon, something horrifying has happened downstairs! – Violette exclaimed.

- What happens?

- Uncle Dunkan has died.

- What? How? Heavens above! What was the cause of his decease?

- It is still unknown. The police is coming.

After he received the bad news, Brandon took his pajamas off and got dressed with the first clothes he found, he washed his face with cold water and coconut essence soap and went downstairs with his sister.

Violette is a thirty-two-year-old woman coming from Portland. She's got a stable relationship with Johnson and three children; Catherine, Megan and George, the youngest. However, their children aren't Johnson's ones. She had the children with Francis, her ex-husband. She and her brother belong to a well-off family that has been settled throughout the West Coast. Her life has been very early. Since she was eighteen, she took the most of the situation. She graduated with honors in law and, of course, she joined the family company. During the years she spent at university, she met his ex-husband and they got married shortly afterwards they finished studying. It seemed that they were the perfect couple. However, she was the only one who knew that it was all over. Francis was too focused on his job as an executive in a big company and he had left his family life aside.

- Violette, Brandon! Come here! – Bob exclaimed.

- We're waiting for you in the living room- the cook said.

- About time! At last you arrive – Bob said.

- What were you doing? – the butler asked in an inquisitive way.

- We took a long time because my brother was very shocked after he knew what happened – Violette stated.

- But, do you feel better now? – the cleaning lady asked.

- Yes, exactly. He is calmer now – Violette replied. Oh! I completely forgot that I was going to call Johnson. I'll do it through the little window in the attic in order to get more range. I don't want the communication to be cut off.

- It isn't going to be so easy because the nearest relay station is at the nearby village, situated four kilometres from here. Besides, it is out of work since last year, when a lightning burnt it – Steve said.

- Anyway, you have nothing to lose by trying – Miss Carroll stated, who was sitting on the red elegant sofa next to the others.

- Are you coming with me, my brother?

- Ok

- However, even if I'm not so hungry, I prefer to have something for breakfast first because it's been too much time since we got up and we haven't eaten anything yet- Violette said.

- I'll prepare something for you – Steve said.

- I also want to have something – Brandon said.

- Will you have a coffee with us, won't you? Violette asked Miss Carroll, Bob and Rodríguez kindly.

- In that case, I'll prepare breakfast for everybody. Would you be so kind as to go to the dining room and have a seat?

A large table completely prepared dominated the dining room, a place that had been witness to a lot of feasts and family meetings for years. It was remarkable that the little details were quite impeccable: the centerpiece with fresh flowers, the glasses and cutlery perfectly organized... it is true that Carroll and Rodríguez have always been very efficient employees. The old Dunkan used to admit that without their help he couldn't live so well in that mansion. After all, he spent so much time with the service, who had become his family since his wife died in that fateful traffic accident in 1995.

Half asleep and a little sad, Violette and Brandon were sitting down. Just after them came Carroll and Rodríguez, feeling a little uncomfortable with the situation. Dunkan loved them as if they were his family but they weren't so close with Violette and Brandon.

- Here you have some pieces of cake made with delicious cow milk from Idaho – Steve said.

- Oh! That's why the taste was familiar to us. Idaho is one of the biggest milk-producing area that supply our city: Portland – Violette stated.

Shyly, they were savoring Steve's cake, which made them almost forget what they were doing there and what had happened. Just the noise of the coffee half made seemed to appear in the dining room.

- Steve, I think the coffee is already made, don't you think so? – Brandon said when he heard the coffee maker creaking again and again.

- Excuse me, but I have to go against you because this coffee is a very special one. In fact, it comes from Indonesia and it is obtained from the excrements of an animal called civet, that's why it needs more time of preparation than a common coffee.

- It should have such a strong taste – Brandon said disgusted.

- It was your uncle's favourite coffee

- Among other things, my uncle has been noted for his culinary pleasures. Not to mention his big generosity helping the most disadvantaged people and other people in general. He was very religious, he loved participating in acts of charity and, of course, if you had any kinds of problems he did everything possible to help you, even if he had to move heaven and earth – Brandon stated with a remarkable upset voice.

\- I don't doubt it. If you'll excuse me, if you don't need anything else, I leave – the butler said.

\- You can leave Rodríguez, should we need anything more, we'll tell you – said Violette cordially.

\- Where are you going? Bob asked.

\- I'm going to my bedroom!

\- Given the circumnstances it is better to go anywhere with someone else and, above all, the home should not be left if it's at all possible. I'll go with you! – the gardener exclaimed insisting.

Bob took a box out of the pocket of his green overalls. He was dressed that way almost all the day because when he isn't cutting the grass, as this horrifying day, he is pruning, defoliating, and occasionally, watering trees, plants and flowers since winters are very cold and there are a lot of precipitations.

In the little box there were two Havana cigars. He took one out of it and, with elegance, he lighted it and started to smoke it while they were going upstairs by the white spiral staircase towards the butler's bedroom.

Bob stopped and felt a weird feeling in his body when he heard an object falling to the floor, which was wrapped in a yellow eye-catching cover. It had an American flag on it, and under it there was a sewing inscription: *I want you for there US Army*.

- We didn't know that you were a soldier, can we know why is it so secret? – Bob asked.

- It is not your business. Now that you know it, if you had a bit of education, you should treat me in a more respectful way because I was an infantry sergeant in the twelfth brigade of this country. I served for more than sixteen years, and the last five ones I was stationed in Spain, specifically in an island called La Palma, which belongs to the Canarian archipelago.

- Sorry but, speaking in geographic terms, where is that group of islands? – the ex firefighter asked with curiosity.

- The island of Lanzarote is the closest to Morocco, in the African continent. They're only separated by ninety-five kilometers of sea. The island where I was is further, in the western zone. These islands are said to be fortunate because of its nice climate. They are influenced by the tradde winds, which blow from the north. That's why they have a warm and mild climate. Moreover, they are into the hourly zone of Greenwich's meridian, in the UK. The last time I was in La Palma was the last month, when I visited some friends from the regiment.

Once in the bedroom, which was between Carroll's one and Bob's one, Rodríguez lied in his bed. Meanwhile, the gardener sat in the edge of the window, from which you could see sideways a partially snowed mountain. The sun, situated on its right, was shining more now.

- Destiny has been particularly cruel to this family. They have had their share of misfortunes. Firstly, Miss Margueritte, who was at a very important moment in her career as a clothes designer when she had that traffic accident. I still remember that twentieth November as if it's today. She was specially happy because she was about to launch her last collection in New York's runway and in that moment she was going to her studio in order to finalize details. And, now, what has happened to Mr. Dunkan. I have a lump in my throat when I think about it – the butler stated.

- It makes my hair stand on end. Nevertheless, I didn't know Miss Margueritte as much as you did. You have worked more time for Mr. Dunkan and his wife.

- It's true. I'm the most veteran, after me Steve arrived, then Miss Carroll and, finally, you – he stressed.

- What's your opinion about Dunkan?

- What do you ask exactly Rodríguez? Are you referring to today's tragedy?

- Exactly.

- It's an atrocity. I don't know what could there be against him to kill him. Well, that is only a supposition. The most probable thing is that he died a natural death, as if it had been a murder, someone would have seen the culprit escape – Bob said.

- It's true, you're right – the butler added.

Later, when they went back to the dining room, they interrumpt the conversation the others were having in that moment, so they asked them what were they talking about. They said they were talking about the awful event since everybody was wondering what could have happened.

Bob and Rodríguez sat down and there were a few minutes' silence. Inmediatly after, Violette went towards the attic to speak to Johnson. As she was going upstairs, she remembered the horrifying cry she had heard, coming from downstairs, when her brother thought it was some racket from last night party, which apparently would have lasted until early morning.

The attic was the deceased favourite room. It was the place where he used to listen to music and read adventure stories in order to relax. As every attic, it received natural light from its dormer window. Under it, there was a eighteen century's bookcase and just in front of it there were a rocking chair and a telescope on the left, to see the stars when the nights were cloudless.

- Hi darling – Violette said.

- Hi my love, good morning, are you still in the mansion?

- That's just what I wanted to tell you. Things are going bad here.

- What happens to you?

- It's not me, it's about uncle Dunkan. The gardener found him dead, lying on the floor, in the limits between the back yard and the garden.

- What? What has happened? I can't believe it. You went there to his birthday party...

- It's true. We don't know what could have happened. It took us by surprise.

- And, how are you? How do you feel?

- I'm sad and confused. You being far from me makes me feel weaker. This is such a difficult situation for me. I also miss my little children, I wonder how they are now.

- Don't worry darling, you'll see that it will solve soon and you'll go back home. Don't worry about the children, they're still in the lake camp – Johnson said trying to calm her.

- Oh Jonhson! Your words make me feel better. I have to leave you because I see someone coming to the mansion – Violette said as she looked through the window.

- It's ok. Call as soon as you know anything else. I love you.

- Me too – Violette replied sighing.

When he opened the door, the butler was able to see the person who was in front of him and who, previously, had knocked at the door. He was the awaited detective, a belly old man who was very smartly dressed. His skin was tanned and his face didn't have a good aspect. However, the most curious thing at all were his bright eyes and his intense look.

Good morning, I'm McArthur the detective, from the Police District. We have received a death notification a few hours ago.

Come in, inspector – the butler said.

I'm aware of the deceased being found by the gardener on the floor.

Yes, you're right.

I'd like to interview the gardener, before going to see the deceased, because he was the first one who found the corpse. That makes him the main suspect.

Go straight on and turn right, there's the dining room where you can find Bob and the others.

Meanwhile, in the living room, they all were expectant as they guessed that the   person who had just arrived came from the Police Department.

Good morning, I'm McArthur the detective. I'd like to talk to the gardener, please.

It's me – Bob said a little surprised.

Leave us alone because he will be the first to be interrogated. Please, everybody should remain in the living room until further notice.

Well, I know that you found Mr. Dunkan, when was it?

At a quarter to eight, this morning.

What were you doing before?

Daily tasks. Today I was cutting the grass. I started with the part of the garden where there is the lumber room, with al the tools. Later, I went back to the kitchen to drink some water and it was then when I saw him.

Could anybody corroborate that you were certainly doing that?

No, I'm afraid not. Early in the morning, everybody is always sleeping. I'm the only one who is awake because I suffer from insomnia and I'm used to wake up very early.

- Could you see any anomalies before the event? Maybe, anybody was behaving in an atypical way? Did you see anybody in the surroundings of the house? The detective interrogated.

- No, I didn't. There wasn't anything unusual. As regards to anybody behaving weirdly, I repeat that everybody was sleeping. As you could check, the house's got high walls around it, so it's very difficult to notice an extranger's presence on the other side of them.

- Tell me, have you always worked for Dunkan?

- No, I haven't. I worked as a firefighter before.

- Well, all the more reason to know that you should cooperate and give us any information to clear up the events – the inspector said finally.

Immediately after, McArthur, accompanied by Bob, went towards the scene of the crime. As he was walking over the red carpet, which had been cleaned that morning he was paying attention to the decorations on the corridor walls, dressed with old candelabra and amazing Rembrandts. Before arriving to the yard, in the end of the corridor, the inspector stopped in the living room and he stressed that they should follow him. Once there, Violette and the others sat in the shade of a green canopy as he approached the corpse in order to examinate it.

- It's curious, there aren't any wounds caused by any weapon. This is not seen even in detective novels where people usually are murdered by the impact of a bullet. Undoubtedly, we are faced with a death by asphyxia.

The layout of arms and legs indicate that there was a struggle between the victim and his executant. The executant threw him on the ground, subdued him and finally used a pillow or a towel to restrict his oxigen intake and his carbon dioxide output through his respiratory tracts. That is why he's got his mouth open and his tongue out of it – the inspector stated while he was walking around the corpse paying attention to every detail.

Although it was clear that the diceased died by asphyxia, McArthur, as a good detective, went on with his investigation, as he still had to investigate who was the perpetrator of the crime. He started to count the steps that there were from the corpse to the lumber room, from the corpse to the yard's door and finally those that were from the corpse to the house wall where there was the window of the butler's room.

- I'm sorry to say it Bob... – said Rodríguez breaking the silence.

-   Say what? What do you hide Bob? – the detective asked.

-   Nothing – Bob answered.

-   I wouldn't say that precisely... – repeated Rodríguez.

-   Owing to the fact that your are reluctant to answer – McArthur said looking to Bob – my only option is to listen to your testimony, Mr Rodríguez. Would you be so kind as to start talking, I'm all ears...

-   Everything happened two weeks ago, when Bob had an unpleasant argument with Mr. Dunkan because of a delay on the monthly payment that he was waiting desperately. With that money he would go to Boston to visit his brother, the only relative he still have – stated the butler.

-   As the investigation goes by I'm finding more reasons and evidences that point out to you as the main culprit Bob, don't you think that having had an argument with the diceased a few weeks ago and you having found the corpse is strange?

- I don'r think it's strange because I simply wasn't who murdered him, it's only a coincidence – the gardener answered with helplessness.

- It will be a coincidence, but it's compromising – said Brandon the nephew.

- Talking about coincidences... I know that you, Brandon, are the second biggest shareholder of a profitable cosmetics company which was managed by your uncle so you could also have important reasons to kill your uncle because you would become the principal shareholder, isn't it true? – the detective asked.

- That is ridiculous, you don't have any evidences of what you say – Brandon answered a little nervous.

- Don't get annoyed Brandon, it's only an hypothesis and in every investigation you have to consider all them. However, I'd like to ask you some questions in private –

McArthur said going towards the living room with Brandon.

Violette was so surprised that she couln't even say a word. His brother, a murderer? She totally refused the idea. She knew that Brandon was ambitious and competitive but he wasn't able even to kill a fly. He loved Dunkan and he said that working with him was very enriching. Both of them were so comfortable working together.

- How long have you been working with your uncle?

- Since only a few months ago because I have just finished my degree in business.

- So, who was Dunkan's right hand man before?

- Mr Dubois.

- Mr Dubois, where do I know that surname from? Oh yes, he must be French or from any colony belonging to France, am I wrong?

- No, you're right. Dubois was parisian. When I arrived I replaced him so he went back to his country.

- Did he and Dunkan get on well?

- I don't know exactly the kinf of relationship they used to have, but I think it wasn't so good as we thought because my uncle offered my the position he had had for almost ten years.

- Confess it, Brandon, I know you killed him. In fact, you are more suspicious than the gardener because if Bob had wanted to kill him, he would have done it before, he wouldn't have waited so much time. Which was the murder's aim, apart from keeping the company? Did you asphyxiated him alone or do you belong to a cell? You've been so clever, you took advantage of everybody being exshausted and asleep after the party to act. Then, you took him out of the bed arguing any problems or simply something important to talk about, you went towards the yard and there you executed him – the detective said so quickly that Brandon couldn't contradict him.

\-   That's enough! Respectfully, I have to tell you that everything you said is grotesque and foolish. You're a trickster who doesn't know how to do his job, well, actually you don't do it! Even though Bob was told that they were going to send their best detective... In short, you leave a lot to be desired as a person and as a professional – Brandon answered tired of insults and lies.

The study was in the end of the corridor, just in front of the bedrooms where Violette and Brandon had atayed last night. As you enter, you can notice the desk's quality and elegance, made with sequoia wood. Behind it there was a bookcase with a staircase to reach the books that were on the top; the sciences and geography ones because those related to business were further down, closer.

The young man took out some cards from his crocodile skin wallet and he looked for a card that a friend of him had given him once. There the name and the phone number of the famous detective Green were written on it.

- Hello, good morning, how can I help you? – Detective Green answered.

- Finally you answer my call, this is the fourth time I try to talk to you. It's of vital importance that you come to the mansion in Ruslake village. Ask the residents where it is, it won't be difficult to find it since it's the only one in the village – Brandon said anxiously.

- Calm down, what's your problem?

- It's about my uncle, he's been murdered this morning. He has been asphyxiated and the police inspector is making false moves, he hasn't stopped of rebuking me and the situation doesn't seem to get better. I'm afraid he will come to the wrong conclusions.

- Well, it's ok, I'll take the next train at eleven o'clock and I'll be arriving in two hours aproximately.

- Thak you for coming, we're waiting for you – Brandon asked a little more calmed.

Meanwhile, McArthur was interrogating Mrs. Carroll in other room.

- It was when everybody was sleeping and the gardener was cutting the grass... ¿isn't it true that you killed him with a clining cloth and then you started to hoove the carpet in order to pass unnoticed? – McArthur inquired.

- It's not true – she answered.

- Yes, of course. That's exactly what the others say – he replied.

Having a look among the things there were on the elegant desk, Brandon stopped at its drawers. The first one was full of bills and papers related to the mansion. He opened the second one and found a big treasure: a pictures album, something that would take him to a trip to the past. He sat in the confortable chair and opened it. On the first page, there were some pictures of him and his sister Violette at Christmas the last year. Undoubtedly, his uncle loved them so much, since they were at the beginning of his collection of souvenirs. He turned a page with curiosity; he couldn't wait for the following pictures. The first ones were in black and white. Although at that time there were in color, Dunkan was very fond of an ancient camera that he treasured.

In those days, Brandon was still four and his sister was a little older. It was then when he and Violette lost their father. That's why Dunkan, their father's brother, took charge of them behaving like a father. At the beginning, they were a bit awkward because of their father's absence. Later, as the time was passing, they learnt to love his uncle. Every year, at their father's death anniversary, they all go to the cemetry to put tulips and anthuriums: his favourite flowers. At that time, memories fill their thoughts and sadness flowers again but, at least, their uncle was supporting them. Moreover, it could be said that thanks to his affection they were able to avoid a traumatic childhood. They used to spend every summer and other school holiday in the mansion. When Violette married George, her ex-husband now, her uncle was the one who gave away the bride.

He turned another page. Absorbed with the trasure, he had forgotten the sad event for a while. The next pictures were already in color. They show the moment when Brandon and Violette were in their teens. Brandon was always a hard-working student who studied easily so he had a lot of free time to do sports, even in winter, as the village had a ski slope. Once he was the third in a national snowboard championship. Violette was the complete opposite of her brother. Despite showing interest and dedication when studying, she didn't have the same gift as Brandon so she used to learn slowly. Dunckan always used to encourange them to study and he used to say that one can never know too much. He knew it very well. Coming from a humble family, he didn't always live with all the comforts of a carefree life. Since he was a child, he used to go everyday to the mountains to take the flock to graze. That's why he only attended the primary school; a short time but he thought it was enough to read and write perfectly. When he was eighteen, his mother gave him some savings, which he spent in a good shoe cleaning kit and he took the streets. He worked and lived in the city for years but since he was limited, due to his low income, he had to sleep in a hostel where he paid one dollar per night. His life changed one day while he was cleaning the shoes of an important businessman. While he was working when he stained accidentally the businessman's sock and trousers with shoe polish. The client flew into a rage and started to discredit Dunkan. He excuse himself stating that he hadn't done it deliberately. He told the businessman that he didn't have much money and he excused himself again. Noticing Dunkan's precarius situation, the businessman offered him a job as a messenger in his company. Since then, Dunkan was promoting gradually until he obtained the necessary money to establish his own company.

Brandon continued seeing the album, which was bringing him so many memories. When he arrived to the end, he breathed deeply and put it away carefully. Then, he went towards the living room to tell her sister the latest news.

- I've called a private detective – Brandon announced with an encouraging voice.

- What for? We already have one from the government. It's a waste of time and money – Rodríguez said.

- On the one hand, it is not your business how much his services cost, since you don't pay for him but I do. On the other hand, a waste of time is how this man does his job – Brandon argued.

- It's true, Rodríguez. He hasn't stopped of accusing us since he arrived, moreover, he hasn't got any evidences – said Bob and Mrs. Carroll almost at the same time.

- In a few hours he'll be here – Brandon said.

- Why don't you solve yourself the case since you seem to be so clever? It isn't simple, it's difficult. One thing at a time – the inspector said.

- How about going to see the greenhouse to show you the flowers and, this way, we calm ourselves a little – Bob suggested.

Everybody nodded except for Brandon, who remained sitting and thinking.

- Be careful or you will slip; the floor is muddy because it has rained the last days. As you can notice, the air we breathe here is much warmer than the air from outside. That is because the plants that I grow need more temperature and humidity – the gardener explained.

He was showing them the rosebushes and chinese carnations while he was talking about their watering frecuency of each species and other related things.

Suddenly, Brandon went towards the main door when he heard the bell ringing.

- Who is it? – Brandon asked.

- It's detective Green – the man answered.

- What? Are you detective Green? – he asked atonished.

- Yes, I am. Why do you ask it?

- Nothing, nothing special. Come in, please. I'm Brandon, the one who called you. Nice to meet you – Brandon said still surprised by the detective's clothes.

Green is a detective who isn't content with being one of the best detectives in the country, he wants to be the number one. He doesn't like his aspect so he doesn't even fix his hair. In fact, he always wears casual clothes even if he goes to an important meeting. He isn't young anymore but he isn't old enough to be considered an old man. He has always worked alone because he never agrees with the rules imposed.

-	The inspector in charge of the case is in the greenhouse with the others – Brandon said.

-	And, what is his name?

-	McArthur.

-	I think I don't know him.

-	Follow me, I'll introduce him to you.

-	Oh no, that will be later. First of all, I want to see the rooms of the house so that I can get on with the job. Show me the way, please.

As Brandon was taking him through the mansion, he was explaining him briefly its structure. After going upstairs, they went first to the bedrooms where he and Violette had slept, which were at the end of the corridor, on the right. Then, they went to Dunkan's bedroom, which was opposite them. On the way to the study and the attic, they passed by the staff rooms.

While Brandon and Green were returning, McArthur and the other were doing the same thing.

- Detective Green, this is Mr. McArthur, the district inspector who is in charge of the case.

- Good afternoon. I greet you to be polite because I don't like at all the presence of other detective in this investigation – McArthur replied as he shook his hand reluctantly.

- Don't worry, I won't interfere in your inquiry, I will investigate in a parallel way because I've been hired to do that – Green replied being less kind now after seeing McArthur's reaction.

- By the way, it's already half past one, take a seat in the dining room, please. I'm serving lunch in a few minutes – the cook said to ease the tension. Then, he went towards the kitchen.

Steve was glad of having cooked too much the day before due to the party as now he will make use of the remaining food to manage the situation. He didn't know that there would be so many people for today's luch and he hadn't had much time during the morning to prepare a succulent meal. He started to serve the food with a modest wine of Dunkan's cellar. A fruit basket would be the dessert that day.

- Who found him? – Green asked while he was cutting an apple.

- Bob, the gardener. He states that he found him on the floor – McArthur answered.

- Didn't anybody hear anything?

- No, nothing at all.

- Everybody seems to sleep deeply, apart from the gardener, who was cutting the grass before the event. Well, it seems that Mrs. Carroll was awake too. After she started cleaning, she saw the gardener moving with impetuosity so she approached, shouted scared and the others came when they heard it.

- What else have you known?

- I know that Brandon could have reasons to kill him because he is the second biggest shareholder of his uncle's company. Mrs. Carroll is also a suspect. Since he died by asphyxia, I think she could have killed him with a cleaning cloth. Although it is clear that Dunkan was stronger than her, so she could have at leat one accomplice.

- Do you see what I mean, detective Green? He's again accusing us withouth evidences – Brandon said.

- If you'll excuse me, I'm leaving. I've already finished. It's already half past two, how time flies! – Green said as he was going towards the scene of the crime.

- He was murdered aproximately – Green calculated looking at his watch – seven hours ago, so neither of the guests killed him because – as Brandon told me – they left the house at 4 a.m. So, the murderer has to be one of the people who are here now in the mansion – Green said talking to himself.

He took out of his leather briefcase a professional camera and started to take pictures of the scene of the crime. Then, he moved the corpse and took out some little plastic bags to gather some samples. He had found a tree leaf hidden among the green grass. He went back to the kitchen and announced that he was leaving to contrast his investigation in another place.

- Then you, Brandon, said that I wasn't on the right track, and this detective you hired doesn't know how to contrast the evidences in situ, assuming that he has found out something new, but in my opinion... – McArthur said boasting about Green's detective skills.

A thoughtful Green went back to the village. He took a taxi at the outskirts and he asked the driver to take him back to the city. Once covered the secondary road and the highway, a lot of tall skyscrapers appeared. The streets were strangely clean and full of people buying in prestigious clothes boutiques or, simply, going for a walk under the shade of the skyscrapers.

- Stop the car! – Green exclaimed.

- It's ninety dollars – the taxi driver said.

- Here you are- the detective said giving him a one hundred dollar bill.

- Hey! Your change! You've got ten dollars left.

- It doesn't matter, keep them for you, I'm in a hurry.

- Would you believe it! Nowadays people don't value money – the taxi driver said having no idea of how much money Green had since he was one of the best detectives in the USA.

Green entered by the green iron door, remarkably rusty by the passage of time. He walked for a long time among the little paths of that green lung situated in the town centre.

- Excuse me, are you the administrator of this botanical garden?

- No, I'm not. I'm one of the assistants.

- Is he here? Could I talk to him a few minutes? I'm detective Green – he added showing him his identification.

- You could have said it before! Come on, follow me!

- Norris, a detective is asking for you – the assistant said while he was opening the door.

- What are you waiting for? Let him come in, don't waste his time.

- Good morning – Green said.

- Good morning. Please, take a seat, I'll be with you in while – the administrator said while he was arranging some papers he had on the desk.

- Could you tell me anything about this leaf? What is its species? – the detective asked as he was putting it on the desk.

- It's a coniferous one, from a pine. If you look carefully, there are three acicular leaves in each leaf sheath. It is a native species from the Canary Islands, specifically from La Palma, El Hierro, Tenerife and Gran

Canaria. Moreover, it comes from the Quaternary period. The canarian pine is the only one in the world that has got three acicular leaves, so definitely this leaf that you show me is from there. Another important characteristic is its resistance to fire. I don't know more than what I have told you – the administrator said.

- Well, thanks – Green said with dismay because he didn't know how to interpret the information.

Green took another taxi to go back to the mansion. He couldn't stop thinking about the information he had just received but he didn't know how to fit it in the investigation's puzzle.

- Hello Violette, I'm back – Green said.

- Hello

- And what? Have you come to arrest the murderer yet? – McArthur asked in a mocking tone.

- Unfortunately not, my investigation hasn't been productive – Green replied with dissapointment.

- In that case, come to the living room, I know who was... – McArthur said.

- Excuse me, before you start talking I would like to ask something. By any chance, has anybody been recently in the Canary Islands, in Spain? – Green asked questioningly.

Everybody looked at themselves and denied it.

- Oh! Rodríguez, you have. You were there a month ago when you went to La Palma to visit your friends of the infantry brigade – said Bob remembering the conversation he had with the butler, who confessed him that he had served for the USA and had been sent some years to La Palma in a mission.

- Tell me Rodríguez, as I understand it, the Canary Islands are known by its beautiful coasts and its natural environment. There is a type of tree very typical there, the pine. By any chance, were there any pines in the surrounding area of the barracks where you stayed at? – Green asked happily.

- Yes, it was surrounded by native pines – Rodriguez asked even if he didn't understand why the detective was talking about all that in that moment.

- Here we have the culprit! – the detective exclaimed as he was explaining to the others that he had found among the grass, next to Dunkan's death body, a canarian pine leaf.

- You! But, how have you been able to kill my uncle? – Brandon said almost couldn't speak.

- You are so cynical, you have been all this time pretending with us when you knew perfectly what had happened – Violette said very nervous.

- Confess it, Rodríguez. You have no way out. The police will arrive in a

few minutes and you'll be arrested –
Green said.

- I... It's true. I did it. A few months
  ago, as I was tidying up Dunkan's
  study I found his will. I kown that I
  shouldn't have read it but I couldn't
  resist the temptation and I did it. I
  realized he hadn't left us anything
  but some letters of introduction. So
  much time working for him and he
  hadn't left me anything! I got furious
  and since then I promised myself that
  I would kill him. I took advantage of
  the party. In the early morning I went
  to his bedroom and I woke him up. I
  told Dunkan that I thought I had seen
  somebody prowling around the yard.
  I asked him to go to have a look and
  when I caught him off guard I threw
  him to the floor and with the jacket I
  was wearing, which I had bought in
  La Palma, I asphyxiated him. I
  thought that this action wouldn't
  leave any trails and I wouldn't be
  found out. It must have happen that,
  unfortunately, a pine leaf got into

one of the pockets and it fell as I was struggling with him.

- See you – Green said victorious, leaving everybody atonished.

www.ingramcontent.com/pod-product-compliance
Lightning Source LLC
LaVergne TN
LVHW010703200726
843507LV00011B/2000